Fireside Al's

TREASURY OF CHRISTMAS STORIES

For our family.

The original paintings for this book
were rendered in oil and acrylic on canvas.

Fireside Al's

TREASURY OF CHRISTMAS STORIES

As Told by
ALAN MAITLAND

With Paintings by
ALAN & LEA DANIEL

Red Deer PRESS

A Fitzhenry & Whiteside Company

"Tribute to Alan Maitland" © 2008 Canadian Broadcasting Corporation

"The Santa Claus Trap" by Margaret Atwood.
Originally published in *Canadian Christmas Stories in Prose and Verse*
edited by Don Bailey and D. Unruh.
© 1990 Margaret Atwood. Reprinted by permission of the Author.

The remaining stories are in the public domain.

5 4 3 2 1

Published by Red Deer Press
A Fitzhenry & Whiteside Company
1512, 1800 – 4 Street SW
Calgary AB T2S 2S5
www.reddeerpress.com

Credits
Audio clips read by Alan Maitland are used courtesy of the Canadian Broadcasting Corporation.
Edited for the Press by Peter Carver
Printed and bound in Canada by Friesens for Red Deer Press

Acknowledgements

Red Deer Press acknowledges the support of the Canada Council for the Arts,
which last year invested $20.1 million in writing and publishing throughout Canada.
Financial support also provided by Government of Canada through the Book
Publishing Industry Development Program (BPIDP).

THE CANADA COUNCIL | LE CONSEIL DES ARTS
FOR THE ARTS | DU CANADA
SINCE 1957 | DEPUIS 1957

Library and Archives Canada Cataloguing in Publication

Fireside Al's treasury of Christmas stories / illustrated by Alan Daniel and Lea Daniel.

Accompanied by CD narrated by Alan Maitland.
ISBN 978-0-88995-382-6

1. Christmas stories, Canadian (English). 2. Christmas stories, American.
3. Christmas stories, English. 4. Canadian fiction (English)—20th century.
5. American fiction—19th century. 6. American fiction—20th century.
7. English fiction—19th century. I. Daniel, Alan, 1939– II. Maitland, Alan

PN6120.95.C6F57 2007   jC813'.0108334   C2007-905319-X

Contents

Yes, Virginia, There Is a Santa Claus   Page 7
Francis P. Church

The Errors of Santa Claus   Page 11
Stephen Leacock

Christmas at Sea   Page 16
Robert Louis Stevenson

To Make a Christmas Cake That Will Keep Until Easter   Page 20
Anonymous

Hoodoo McFiggin's Christmas   Page 22
Stephen Leacock

The Santa Claus Trap   Page 27
Margaret Atwood

The Gift of the Magi   Page 43
O. Henry

The Trapper's Christmas Eve   Page 52
Robert W. Service

The First Christmas Tree   Page 56
Eugene Field

A Tribute to Alan Maitland   Page 64

Yes, Virginia, There Is a Santa Claus

FRANCIS P. CHURCH

It's autumn, 1898. The rain beats against the tightly closed windows of the old brownstone houses, and the first of the season's Atlantic gales swoops down the broad streets and eddies around the tall buildings. A small girl sits in a cozy bedroom, her head on her hands, staring out at the gathering dusk and the bitter weather. She is thinking about Christmas. You may think, my friends, that the onset of autumn is a touch early to be thinking of Christmas. But this small girl is perplexed.

Virginia O'Hanlon lives in New York City in a comfortable house in a pleasant area on West 95th. She is eight years old, and goes to school, and every day she learns something new about the world. Today one of her friends told Virginia that there is no Santa Claus, and she's troubled. If there is no Santa Claus, what is to become of Christmas? This is a loss that can scarcely be contemplated. So Virginia goes downstairs to talk to her father who is reading in his den, smoking a pipe in front of a blazing fire. He listens gravely and like all parents, dear listeners, finds himself at a loss for words when faced with the real questions of life. So, gently, he suggests that Virginia should write a letter to the editors of the newspaper and ask those wise and articulate men about her problem.

Immediately Virginia goes to her room and carefully prints the following letter to the editors of the *New York Sun*.

Dear Editor:
I am eight years old. Some of my little friends say there is
no Santa Claus. Papa says: "If you see it in the *Sun*, it is so."
Please tell me the truth. Is there a Santa Claus?
Virginia O'Hanlon,
115 West 95th Street,
New York City

The letter sits on the desk of a tough old city editor. Every now and then he picks it up and looks around for a junior reporter, intending to pass the childish note to a subordinate for a quick and routine answer. But something keeps stopping him. He's not a man given to sentiment, having no children nor a wife, and a childhood that gets more remote every year. But this letter disturbs him. He pushes his hat back on his head and relights his cigar. By now he's almost alone in the newsroom. He reaches into the recesses of his rolltop desk and finds a bottle of whiskey and pours himself a shot. He drinks reflectively, looking back on two score years of unspecial Christmases and, before, those magic days of childhood when Christmas was the brightest moment of the year, better by far than birthdays.

Deadline is getting near. "Doggone it," says the crusty old editor. He stubs his cigar in the overflowing ashtray, takes another pull on his drink, and swivels his chair abruptly to the battered typewriter. He rams in a piece of paper, and furiously starts to type.

The next day, the *New York Sun* ran the following editorial.

Virginia, your little friends are wrong. They have been affected by the skepticism of a skeptical age. They do not believe except they see. They think that nothing can be which is not comprehensible by their

little minds. All minds, Virginia, whether they be men's or children's, are little. In this great universe of ours, man is a mere insect, an ant, in his intellect as compared with the boundless world about him, as measured by the intelligence capable of grasping the whole of truth and knowledge.

Yes, Virginia, there is a Santa Claus. He exists as certainly as love and generosity and devotion exist, and you know that they abound and give to your life its highest beauty and joy. Alas! how dreary would be the world if there were no Santa Claus! It would be as dreary as if there were no Virginias. There would be no childlike faith then, no poetry, no romance to make tolerable this existence. We should have no enjoyment, except in sense and sight. The eternal light with which childhood fills the world would be extinguished.

Not believe in Santa Claus! You might as well not believe in fairies. You might get your papa to hire men to watch in all the chimneys on Christmas Eve to catch Santa Claus, but even if they did not see Santa Claus coming down, what would that prove? Nobody sees Santa Claus, but that is no sign that there is no Santa Claus. The most real things in the world are those that neither children nor men see. Did you ever see fairies dancing on the lawn? Of course not, but that's no proof that they are not there. Nobody can conceive or imagine all the wonders there are unseen and unseeable in the world.

You tear apart the baby's rattle and see what makes the noise inside, but there is a veil covering the unseen world which not the strongest man, nor even the united strength of all the strongest men that ever lived could tear apart. Only faith, fancy, poetry, love, romance, can push aside that curtain and view and picture the supernal beauty and glory beyond. Is it all real? Oh, Virginia, in all this world there is nothing else real and abiding.

No Santa Claus! Thank God he lives and he lives forever. A thousand years from now, Virginia, nay 10,000 years from now, he will continue to make glad the heart of childhood.

The Errors of Santa Claus

STEPHEN LEACOCK

It was Christmas Eve.

The Browns, who lived in the adjoining house, had been dining with the Joneses. Brown and Jones were sitting over wine and walnuts at the table. The others had gone upstairs.

"What are you giving your boy for Christmas?" asked Brown.

"A train," said Jones, "new kind of thing—automatic."

"Let's have a look at it," said Brown.

Jones fetched a parcel from the sideboard and began unwrapping it.

"Ingenious thing, isn't it?" he said. "Goes on its own rails. Queer how kids love to play with trains, isn't it?"

"Yes," assented Brown. "How are the rails fixed?"

"Wait, I'll show you," said Jones. "Just help me to shove these dinner things aside and roll back the cloth. There! See! You lay the rails like that and fasten them at the ends, so…"

"Oh, yeah, I catch on, makes a grade, doesn't it? Just the thing to amuse a child, isn't it? I got Willy a toy aeroplane."

"I know, they're great. I got Edwin one on his birthday. But I thought I'd get him a train this time. I told him Santa Claus was going to bring him something altogether new this time. Edwin, of course, believes in Santa Claus absolutely. Say, look at this locomotive, would you? It has a spring coiled up inside the firebox."

"Wind her up," said Brown with great interest. "Let's see her go."

"All right," said Jones. "Just pile up two or three plates, as something to lean the end of the rails on. There, notice the way it buzzes before it starts. Isn't that a great thing for a kid, eh?"

"Yes," said Brown. "And say, see this little string to pull the whistle! By Gad, it toots, eh? Just like real?"

"Now then, Brown," Jones went on, "you hitch on those cars and I'll start her. I'll be engineer, eh!"

Half an hour later Brown and Jones were still playing trains on the dining room table.

But their wives upstairs in the drawing room hardly noticed their absence. They were too much interested.

"Oh, I think it's perfectly sweet," said Mrs. Brown. "Just the loveliest doll I've seen in years. I must get one like it for Ulvina. Won't Clarisse be perfectly enchanted?"

"Yes," answered Mrs. Jones, "and then she'll have all the fun of arranging the dresses. Children love that so much. Look, there are three little dresses with the doll—aren't they cute? All cut out and ready to stitch together."

"Oh, how perfectly lovely!" exclaimed Mrs. Brown. "I think the mauve one would suit the doll best, don't you, with such golden hair? Only don't you think it would make it much nicer to turn back the collar, so, and put a little band—so?"

"*What* a good idea!" said Mrs. Jones. "Do let's try it. Just wait, I'll get a needle in a minute. I'll tell Clarisse that Santa Claus sewed it himself. The child believes in Santa Claus absolutely."

And half an hour later Mrs. Jones and Mrs. Brown were so busy stitching dolls' clothes that they could not hear the roaring of the little train up and down the dining table, and had no idea what the four children were doing.

Nor did the children miss their mothers.

"Dandy, aren't they?" Edwin Jones was saying to little Willie Brown, as they sat in Edwin's bedroom. "A hundred in a box, with cork tips, and see, an amber mouthpiece that fits into a little case at the side. Good present for Dad, eh?"

"Fine!" said Willie appreciatively. "I'm giving Father cigars."

"I know, I thought of cigars too. Men always like cigars and cigarettes. You can't go wrong on them. Say, would you like to try one or two of these cigarettes? We can take them from the bottom. You'll like them, they're Russian—away ahead of Egyptian."

"Thanks," answered Willie. "I'd like one immensely. I only started smoking last spring—on my twelfth birthday. I think a feller's a fool to begin smoking cigarettes too soon, don't you? It stunts him. I waited till I was twelve."

"Me too," said Edwin, as they lighted their cigarettes. "In fact, I wouldn't buy them now if it weren't for Dad. I simply *had* to give him something from Santa Claus. He believes in Santa Claus absolutely."

And, while this was going on, Clarisse was showing little Ulvina the absolutely lovely little bridge set that she got for her mother.

"Aren't these markers perfectly charming?" said Ulvina. "And don't you love this little Dutch design—or is it Flemish, darling?"

"Dutch," said Clarisse. "Isn't it quaint? And aren't these the dearest little things, for putting the money in when you play. I needn't have got them with it—they'd have sold the rest separately—but I think it's too utterly slow playing without money, don't you?"

"Oh, abominable," shuddered Ulvina. "But your mamma never plays for money, does she?"

"Mamma! Oh, gracious, no. Mamma's far too slow for that. But I shall tell her that Santa Claus insisted on putting in the little money boxes."

"I suppose she believes in Santa Claus, just as my mamma does."

"Oh, absolutely," said Clarisse, and added, "What if we play a little game! With a double dummy, the French way, or Norwegian Skat, if you like. That only needs two."

"All right," agreed Ulvina, and in a few minutes they were deep in a game of cards with a little pile of pocket money beside them.

About half an hour later, all the members of the two families were down again in the drawing room. But of course nobody said anything about the presents. In any case they were all too busy looking at the beautiful big Bible, with maps in it, that the Joneses had brought to give to Grandfather. They all agreed that, with the help of it, Grandfather could hunt up any place in Palestine in a moment, day or night.

But upstairs, away upstairs in a sitting room of his own, Grandfather Jones was looking with an affectionate eye at the presents that stood beside him. There was a beautiful whiskey decanter, with silver filigree outside (and whiskey inside) for Jones, and for the little boy a big nickel-plated Jew's harp.

Later on, far into the night, the person, or the influence, or whatever it is called Santa Claus, took all the presents and placed them in the people's stockings.

And, being blind as he always has been, he gave the wrong things to the wrong people—in fact, he gave them just as indicated above.

But the next day, in the course of Christmas morning, the situation straightened itself out, just as it always does.

Indeed, by ten o'clock, Brown and Jones were playing with the train, and Mrs. Brown and Mrs. Jones were making dolls' clothes, and the boys were smoking cigarettes, and Clarisse and Ulvina were playing cards for their pocket money.

And upstairs—away up—Grandfather was drinking whiskey and playing the Jew's harp.

And so Christmas, just as it always does, turned out all right after all.

Christmas at Sea

ROBERT LOUIS STEVENSON

The sheets were frozen hard, and they cut the naked hand;
The decks were like a slide, where a seamen scarce could stand;
The wind was a nor'wester, blowing squally off the sea;
And cliffs and spouting breakers were the only things alee.
They heard the surf a-roaring before the break of day;
But 'twas only with the peep of light we saw how ill we lay.
We tumbled every hand on deck instanter, with a shout,
And we gave her the maintops'l, and stood by to go about.

All day we tacked and tacked between the South Head and the North;
All day we hauled the frozen sheets, and got no further forth;
All day as cold as charity, in bitter pain and dread,
For very life and nature we tacked from head to head.

We gave the South a wider berth, for there the tide-race roared;
But every tack we made we brought the North Head close aboard:
So's we saw the cliffs and houses, and the breakers running high,
And the coastguard in his garden, with his glass against his eye.

The frost was on the village roofs as white as ocean foam;
The good red fires were burning bright in every longshore home;
The windows sparkled clear, and the chimneys volleyed out;
And I vow we sniffed the victuals as the vessel went about.

The bells upon the church were rung with a mighty jovial cheer;
For it's just that I should tell you how (of all days in the year)
This day of our adversity was blessed Christmas morn,
And the house above the coastguard's was the house where I was
     born.

O well I saw the pleasant room, the pleasant faces there,
My mother's silver spectacles, my father's silver hair;
And well I saw the firelight, like a flight of homely elves,
Go dancing round the china plates that stand upon the shelves.

And well I knew the talk they had, the talk that was of me,
Of the shadow on the household and the son that went to sea;
And O the wicked fool I seemed, in every kind of way,
To be here and hauling frozen ropes on blessed Christmas Day.

They lit the high sea light, and the dark began to fall.
"All hands to loose topgallant sails," I heard the captain call.
"By the Lord, she'll never stand it," our first mate, Jackson, cried.
"It's the one way or the other, Mr. Jackson," he replied.

She staggered to her bearings, but the sails were new and good,
And the ship smelt up to windward just as though she understood.
As the winter's day was ending, in the entry of the night,
We cleared the weary headland, and passed below the light.

And they heaved a mighty breath, every soul on board but me,
As they saw her nose again pointing handsome out to sea;
But all that I could think of, in the darkness and the cold,
Was just that I was leaving home and my folks were growing old.

To Make a Christmas Cake That Will Keep Until Easter

ANONYMOUS

A recipe from 1709

TAKE FOUR POUNDS OF BUTTER, break it in a pan and work it well with your hands 'til it comes to a cream.

THEN TAKE A QUART OF ALE YEAST, strain it into the butter, and still keep working it.

THEN, TAKE THE YOLKS OF TEN EGGS and beat them and put to them half a pint of rose water or orange flower water and almost a quart of cream, and strain them in the butter and yeast, but cease not working on it 'til you put it to the hoop.

THEN, TAKE HALF A PECK OF THE FINEST FLOUR and a pound of loaf sugar, beaten fine, and a quart of an ounce of mace, beaten and mingled with the flour.

WHEN YOU HAVE WORKED ALL VERY WELL TOGETHER, so that you have made it soft again with your working, then put half your flour and work well together; then take six pounds of currants, picked, washed and dried, and mingled with the rest of the flour and, by degrees, put them to the butter and work them very well in it, so that they be very well mingled in it.

YOUR CAKE MUST BE AS STIFF, as it will stick about the pan and your hands.

SET IT IN THE OVEN, then heat a little batter, and let it stand two hours or more.

Hoodoo McFiggin's Christmas

STEPHEN LEACOCK

This Santa Claus business is played out. It's a sneaking, underhand method, and the sooner it's exposed the better.

For a parent to get up under cover of darkness and palm off a ten-cent necktie on a boy who had been expecting a ten-dollar watch, and then say that an angel sent it to him, is low, undeniably low.

I had the good opportunity of observing how the thing worked this Christmas, in the case of young Hoodoo McFiggin, the son and heir of the McFiggins, at whose house I board.

Hoodoo McFiggin is a good boy—a religious boy. He had been given to understand that Santa Claus would bring nothing to his father and mother because grown-up people didn't get presents from the angels. So he saved up all his pocket money and bought a box of cigars for his father and a seventy-five-cent diamond brooch for his mother. His own fortunes he left in the hands of the angels. But he prayed. He prayed every night for weeks that Santa Claus would bring him a pair of skates and a puppy dog and an air gun and a bicycle and a Noah's ark and a sleigh and a drum—altogether about a hundred and fifty dollars' worth of stuff.

I went into Hoodoo's room quite early Christmas morning. I had an idea that the scene would be interesting. I woke him up and he sat up in bed, his eyes glistening with radiant expectation, and began hauling things out of his stocking.

The first parcel was bulky; it was done up quite loosely and had an odd look generally.

"Ha! Ha!" Hoodoo cried gleefully, as he began undoing it. "I'll bet it's the puppy dog, all wrapped up in paper!"

And was it the puppy dog? No, by no means. It was a pair of nice, strong, number four boots, laces and all, labelled: *Hoodoo, from Santa Claus*, and underneath Santa Claus had written, *Ninety-five cents net*.

The boy's jaw fell with delight. "It's boots," he said, and plunged in his hand again.

He began hauling away at another parcel with renewed hope on his face.

This time the thing seemed like a little round box. Hoodoo tore the paper off with a feverish hand. He shook it; something rattled inside.

"It's a watch and chain! It's a watch and chain!" he said. Then he pulled the lid off.

And was it a watch and chain? No. No, it was a box of nice, brand new celluloid collars, a dozen of them all alike, all his own size.

The boy was so pleased that you could see his face crack up with pleasure.

He waited a few minutes until his intense joy subsided. Then he tried again. This time the packet was long and hard. It resisted the touch and had a sort of funnel shape.

"It's a toy pistol!" said the boy, "it's a toy pistol! Gee! I hope there are lots of caps with it! I'll fire some off now and wake up Father."

No, my poor child, you will not wake your father with that. It is a

useful thing, but it needs not caps and it fires no bullets, and you cannot wake a sleeping man with a toothbrush. Yes, yes, it was a toothbrush—a regular beauty, pure bone all through, and ticketed with a little paper: *Hoodoo, from Santa Claus.*

Again the expression of intense joy passed over the boy's face, and the tears of gratitude started from his eyes. He wiped them away with his toothbrush and passed on.

The next packet was much larger and evidently contained something soft and bulky. It had been too long to go into the stocking and was tied outside.

"I wonder what this is," Hoodoo mused, half afraid to open it. Then his heart gave a great leap, and he forgot all his other presents in the anticipation of this one. "It's a drum," he gasped, "it's a drum, all wrapped up!"

Drum nothing! It was pants—a pair of the nicest little short pants—yellowish-brown short pants—with dear little strips of colour running across both ways, and here again Santa Claus had written: *Hoodoo, from Santa Claus, one forty net.*

But there was something wrapped up in it. Oh, yes! There was a pair of braces wrapped up in it, braces with a little steel sliding thing so that you could slide your pants up to your neck, if you wanted to.

The boy gave a dry sob of satisfaction. Then he took out his last present. "It's a book," he said, "it's a book! I wonder if it is fairy stories or adventures. Oh, I hope it's adventures! I'll read it all morning."

No, Hoodoo, it was not precisely adventures. It was a small family Bible. Hoodoo had now seen all his presents, and he arose and dressed. But he still had the fun of playing with his toys. That is always the chief delight of Christmas morning.

First he played with his toothbrush. He got a whole lot of water and brushed all his teeth with it. This was huge.

Then he played with his collars. He had no end of fun with them, taking them all out one by one and swearing at them, and then putting them back and swearing at the whole lot together.

The next toy was his pants. He had immense fun there, putting them on and taking them off again, and then trying to guess which side was which by merely looking at them.

After that he took his book and read some adventures called *Genesis* till breakfast-time.

Then he went downstairs, and kissed his father and mother. His father was smoking a cigar, and his mother had her new brooch on. Hoodoo's face was thoughtful, and a light seemed to have broken in upon his mind. Indeed, I think it altogether likely that next Christmas he will hang on to his own pocket money and take chances on what the angels bring.

The Santa Claus Trap

MARGARET ATWOOD

Once upon a time there was a man named Mr. Grate,
Whom the thought of Christmas filled
With an indescribable and fungoid hate.

He hated Christmas trees and presents
And carols and turkeys and plum
Puddings, and he thought Santa Claus and his reindeer
Were not only dumb

But ought to be banned and not allowed
Into the country, and dogs
That barked and children who laughed
Too much made him furious,
And he wished they would all fall down
Holes or drown in bogs.

Mr. Grate, although he was quite rich,
Lived in one miserable little room
Which he never cleaned with a vacuum cleaner
Or swept with a broom

So that it was all covered with dust and dirt
And spiderwebs and old pieces of cheese
And so was Mr. Grate,
And if you ever came near him
You would begin to cough and sneeze,

But nobody ever did, because he never went outside,
But stayed in,
And counted his money, and wrote nasty letters to the editor,
And sometimes drank a bottle of gin

All by himself, or a glass of lemonade without any sugar,
Because he liked it sour,
And he peered out the window and hated everybody,
By the hour.

He had round eyes like an owl's
And his face was all squizzled up
And covered with frowns and scowls.

One day in December, Mr. Grate thought up a horrible plot.
"Everyone," he said to himself—he talked out loud a lot—
"Has a lot of nice things, much nicer than anything *I've* got,

And every Christmas they give each other presents,
And nobody ever gives *me* none,
And not only that, but I never have any fun,

And Santa Claus comes and fills their stockings
And panti-hose and socklets
With oranges and licorice sticks and bubble gum
And chocolates.

But what if Santa Claus were to suddenly disappear,
And all that ever gets found is his empty sled and reindeer?
What if I could kidnap Santa Claus and keep him in a sack
And say I would never give him back

Unless the children sent ME all their candy
And jellybeans and maybe a teddy bear?
Not only would I get even with them and give them a scare,
But I'd have all the stuff, and maybe I'd even be a millionaire.

I'll keep Santa Claus in a cupboard
And feed him on water and crumbs,
While I sit outside and laugh myself silly
And stuff myself with candy apples and bubble gums!"

And for the first time in a long long while,
Mr. Grate began to laugh and chuckle,
But it wasn't a nice laugh, and he turned all red and purple
And rolled around on the floor
And had to loosen his belt buckle.

After that he got up again and set to work.
"The thing is," he said to himself,
"Santa Claus is obviously a jerk:

All he ever does is give things to people—
It's really shocking—
And he can't seem to resist an unfilled stocking.

Therefore, all I have to do is get a lot of stockings,
And hang them all over the room as a kind of bait,
And build a trap in the fireplace that will catch him
When he comes down the chimney,
And then I'll just sit and wait."

So first Mr. Grate went to a Sale,
And bought a whole armful of stockings
And socks and mukluks and several rubber boots,
Pushing old ladies out of his way
And scowling and frowning at the men
Who were ringing bells, dressed up in Santa Claus suits,

And then he went to a junk yard and bought all kinds of junk:
Some pieces of old cars, a wringer washing machine,
Several rolls of barbed wire,
Some string and rubber bands, a wrench, a lever, a gear,
And a box full of old tin cans
Which unfortunately also contained a dead skunk,

But that's life, said Mr. Grate to himself
As he carted all these things home
In a U-Haul he'd rented.
And when he got them back to his room, he started to build
The most complicated trap that has ever been invented.

The trap was foolproof and full of pulleys and levers,
And anyone who came down the chimney and stepped into it
Would be grabbed by mechanical hands
And rollered on rollers and tangled in wires and zoomed
Right into a sack in Mr. Grate's closet,
And it looked as if Santa Claus was doomed,

EXCEPT

Next door to Mr. Grate lived some twins,
A girl named Charlotte and a boy named William.
Charlotte's favourite flower was the Rose,
And William's was the Trillium.

They were both very curious
And they were always looking in people's windows
And back yards and bureau drawers or over their shoulders.
Charlotte was somewhat self-contained,
But William was bolder.

And one day, when Mr. Grate was building his trap and
Talking out loud to himself
About his plan to hold Santa Claus to ransom,
Charlotte just happened to be standing on William's shoulders
And looking through his transom.

She overheard the whole plan, and she was so dismayed
She almost fell off,
And then she almost gave them away,
Because even Mr. Grate's transom was so dusty
It made her cough,

But luckily Mr. Grate was hammering something
At the time, and didn't hear.
Charlotte climbed down and whispered in William's ear,
"William, I have just heard the most terrible thing,
And Christmas is going to be ruined this year!"
These words of Charlotte's filled William's heart with fear.

The twins hurried back to their own house,
And sat down at the kitchen table,
And while they were eating some peanut butter sandwiches
To keep up their strength,
Charlotte repeated what she had heard, as well as she was able.
"But that's terrible!" said William. "If Santa Claus is caught
In the trap, and tied up with a large knot,

No children in the entire world
Will get anything in their stockings, you see!
And—I hardly need to point out—

That includes you and me.
I feel that this could turn into a major catastrophe."

"Don't be so obvious," Charlotte said.
"The main thing is, how can we stop him?"
"Well," said William,
"I could go over there with my baseball bat and bop him
On the head." "You aren't big enough,"
Charlotte said, she was practical.
"We have to think of a plan that is both feasible and tactical,

By which I mean something we can do ourselves
That will actually work."
But the possibility of no Santa Claus
Filled them with depression, gloom, and murk,

And they found it hard to even think about it,
It made them so sad.
"Some people are naughty," said Charlotte,
"But Mr. Grate is *bad*."

For days they did nothing but sigh and mutter
And eat sandwiches made of peanut butter.

Once they went to spy on Mr. Grate,
But the trap was even bigger,
And Mr. Grate was rubbing his hands
And looking at it, with a nasty snigger.

The sight of the enormous trap
Made Charlotte and William feel helpless and small,
And they seemed unable to think of anything to do at all.

They knew they couldn't tell the police or any grownups,
Because no one would believe them anyway,
And it was too late to write Santa Claus to warn him,
Because Christmas was due now any day.

"Is this the end?" said William, feeling doleful.
"Do not give up," said Charlotte, looking soulful.

AT LAST

They had a brilliant idea, and being twins
They had it both at once, because
Twins often do. "I know!" they cried together.
"We'll make a false Santa Claus!

We'll make it out of red potato sacks, and fill it full of rocks,
And let it down Mr. Grate's chimney on a rope,
And it will snarl up the trap and possibly break it, because
Of the rocks." This idea filled them with hope.

"Come on," said William, "let's get going,
We have no time to waste!"
So, pausing only to eat one more small sandwich each
And to put on their winter coats
And their mittens, boots and hats,
They rushed out the door in considerable haste.

"Where are they going?"
Their mother called after them as they ran down the street.
"We're going to save Santa Claus!" they called back, and
Not realizing the seriousness of the situation,
She said, "Isn't that sweet."

It was Christmas Eve, and Mr. Grate
Had hung up his stocking, or should I say
His stockings, because he had about a hundred of them
Dangling all over his room,
In every colour you can think of,
Red, green, yellow, purple, blue, and gray,
And the total effect would have been rather joyous and gay

If it hadn't been for the sinister machine
Lurking near the fireplace in the corner.
"All right, Santa Claus," muttered Mr. Grate,
"Once down that chimney and you're a goner!"

He was sitting in his one dingy old chair,
Hugging himself and chortling,
When up on his roof he heard an odd sound,
Part scuffling and part snortling.

"It must be a reindeer!" cried Mr. Grate, and jumped up
To give the final touch to his arrangement of socks.
(It was actually Charlotte and William,
Having a little trouble with the rocks.)

"Now Santa will slide down the chimney
With a nice, round, fat kind of slither,
And I'll have him safe in my closet,
And all the children of the world will be thrown into a dither,
And serve them right," said Mr. Grate.
He could hardly wait.

But imagine his surprise
When instead of a round little man landing
With a comfortable plop in his trap, there was a loud crash!
Followed by a thud and a rattle and a smash!

Someone—or something—dressed in red
Had come down the chimney, though it wasn't light

Enough to see clearly, and Mr. Grate's trap had spun into action,
But it was throwing out sparks left and right!

Its mechanical arms were getting all snarled up
In the barbed wire,
And its washing machine wringer was out of control,
Spinning higher and higher,
And something seemed to be wrong
With the sack that Santa was supposed to fall into—
It had caught on fire!

Suddenly all the fuses blew,
And a thin, tiny, eerie voice came wafting
Down the chimney flue:

"Mr. Grate! Mr. Grate!

REPENT

Before it is too late."

This was actually Charlotte,
Which Mr. Grate had no way of knowing.
"It's ghosts!" he cried.
"I've got to get out of here, even though it's snowing!"

He ran towards the door, but because
There were now no lights in the entire place,
He tripped over something and fell flat on his face.

Then something else grabbed him from behind,
And one of the gears that wasn't broken began to grind,

And then there was an unpleasant ZAP
And Mr. Grate was caught in his own trap!
"Help! Help," he cried, and began to struggle,
Which only made the tangle worse,
"I'm perishing! I'm expiring!
I need a doctor and also a nurse! O curse

The day I decided to trap poor Santa Claus!
Please, someone, bring some wire clippers and tin-snips,
And wrenches, and saws
And get me out!"

Charlotte and William, on the roof, heard his feeble shout.
"I believe it's worked," Charlotte said. "He seems to be caught,
Which is more than we expected.
Should we let him out, or not?"

Mr. Grate was lying all covered with barbed wire
And bits of cheese from the floor,
And feeling decidedly sorry for himself,
And also rather battered and sore,
When Charlotte and William climbed
Through the transom over his door.

(They didn't have a key, and the door itself was locked.)
"Well," said Charlotte, looking down at Mr. Grate,
Where he lay clinking and clanking,
"In my opinion you deserve a good spanking."

"In *my* opinion," said William,
"You deserve a good kick in the behind."
"But," said Charlotte, intervening—
She felt one should be polite, if at all possible—
"This is Christmas and we are going to be kind.

We'll get you out of the trap *this* time,
If you promise not to do it again, and make amends."
"But why did you think of such an evil thing to do
In the first place?" said William.
"Boohoo," said Mr. Grate, "I don't have any friends,

Or a teddy bear, or *anything*,
And everyone else was having such a good time,
Especially at Christmas, and my room is all covered with grime,
And no one invites me to dinner,

And I never get anything in my stocking but pieces of coal,
Or sometimes a hole,
Or a rotten potato, and once, in a good year, a single Smartie,
And it's a long long time since I even went to a birthday party!"

"There, there," said Charlotte, wiping away his grubby tears,
While William was snipping him out of the trap
With a pair of shears,

"I understand perfectly. You just wanted some attention."
(Which had been said to her on several occasions
When she herself had been rather surly,
But these we won't mention.)

"You can come back to *our* house for Christmas.
I'm sure our Mum won't mind, if we ask,
And we'll even help you clean up your room."
Which they did, and it was an unpleasant task…

But in Mr. Grate's closet they found a couple of suits
That weren't too dirty,
And when they had washed his face and shined his boots

He looked quite presentable,
And was so pleased he actually smiled
And allowed his fingernails to be cut and his moustache filed,

And off they all went to Charlotte's and William's house,
And had a wonderful Christmas dinner
With lots of trimmings,
And when Mr. Grate got up from the table
He was certainly not thinner.

And after that day, though he was not
A completely different person, and still
Didn't like dogs much, and was known to spill

A few bits of cheese on the carpet now and then,
He was much nicer than before,
And played Monopoly with Charlotte and William,
So that they were quite glad he lived next door.

And he changed the spelling of his name to Mr. Great,
And often said things like "It's never too late."

"And although he didn't manage
To *catch* Santa Claus," said Charlotte one day,
"At least he *found* him."
Which is true, when you think about it, in a way,

And also he had found not only one friend
But two. Which is a pretty good place to say

THE END.

The Gift of the Magi

O. Henry

One dollar and eighty-seven cents. That was all. And sixty cents of it was in pennies. Pennies saved one and two at a time by bulldozing the grocer and the vegetable man and the butcher until one's cheeks burned with the silent imputation of parsimony that such close dealing implied. Three times Della counted it. One dollar and eighty-seven cents. And the next day would be Christmas.

There was clearly nothing to do but flop down on the shabby little couch and howl. So Della did it. Which instigates the moral reflection that life is made up of sobs, sniffles, and smiles, with sniffles predominating.

While the mistress of the home is gradually subsiding from the first stage to the second, take a look at the home. A furnished flat at eight dollars per week. It did not exactly beggar description, but it certainly had that word on the lookout for the mendicancy squad.

In the vestibule below was a letter box into which no letter would go, and an electric button from which no mortal finger could coax a ring. Also appertaining thereto was a card bearing the name, "Mr. James Dillingham Young."

The "Dillingham" had been flung to the breeze during a former period of prosperity when its possessor was being paid thirty dollars per week. Now, when the income was shrunk to twenty dollars, the letters of "Dillingham" looked blurred as though they were thinking seriously of contracting to a modest and unassuming "D." But whenever Mr. James Dillingham Young came home and reached his flat above he was called "Jim" and greatly hugged by Mrs. James Dillingham Young, already introduced to you as Della. Which is all very good.

Della finished her cry and attended to her cheeks with the powder puff. She stood by the window and looked out dully at a grey cat walking a grey fence in a grey backyard. Tomorrow would be Christmas Day, and she had only one dollar and eighty-seven cents with which to buy Jim a present. She had been saving every penny she could for months, with this result. Twenty dollars a week doesn't go far. Expenses had been greater than she had calculated. They always are. Only one dollar and eighty-seven cents to buy a present for Jim. Her Jim. Many a happy hour she had spent planning for something nice for him. Something fine and rare and sterling—something just a little bit near to being worthy of the honour of being owned by Jim.

There was a pier glass between the windows of the room. Perhaps you have seen a pier glass in an eight-dollar flat. A very thin and very agile person may, by observing his reflection in a rapid sequence of longitudinal strips, obtain a fairly accurate conception of his looks. Della, being slender, had mastered the art.

Suddenly she whirled from the window and stood before the glass. Her eyes were shining brilliantly, but her face had lost its colour within twenty seconds. Rapidly she pulled down her hair and let it fall to its full length.

Now, there were two possessions of the James Dillingham Youngs in which they both took a mighty pride. One was Jim's gold watch

that had been his father's and his grandfather's. The other was Della's hair. Had the queen of Sheba lived in the flat across the airshaft, Della would have let her hair hang out the window someday to dry just to depreciate Her Majesty's jewels and gifts. Had King Solomon been the janitor, with all his treasures piled up in the basement, Jim would have pulled out his watch every time he passed, just to see him pluck at his beard from envy.

So now Della's beautiful hair fell about her, rippling and shining like a cascade of brown waters. She did it up again nervously and quickly. Once she faltered for a minute and stood still while a tear or two splashed on the worn red carpet.

On went her old brown jacket; on went her old brown hat. With a whirl of skirts and with the brilliant sparkle still in her eyes, she fluttered out the door and down the stairs to the street.

Where she stopped the sign read: *Mme. Sofronie. Hair Goods of All Kinds.* One flight up Della ran, and collected herself, panting. Madame, large, too white, chilly, hardly looked the "Sofronie."

"Will you buy my hair?" asked Della.

"I buy hair," said Madame. "Take yer hat off and let's have a sight at the looks of it."

Down rippled the brown cascade.

"Twenty dollars," said Madame, lifting the mass with a practised hand.

"Give it to me quick," said Della.

Oh, and the next two hours tripped by on rosy wings. Forget the hashed metaphor. She was ransacking the stores for Jim's present.

She found it at last. It surely had been made for Jim and no one else. There was no other like it in any of the stores, and she had turned all of them inside out. It was a platinum watch chain simple and chaste in design, properly proclaiming its value by substance alone and not by meretricious ornamentation—as all good things should do. It was even worthy of The Watch. As soon as she saw it she knew that it must be Jim's. It was like him. Quietness and value—the description applied to both. Twenty-one dollars they took from her for it, and she hurried home with the eighty-seven cents. With that chain on his watch Jim might be properly anxious about the time in any company. Grand as the watch was, he sometimes looked at it on the sly on account of the old leather strap that he used in place of a chain.

When Della reached home her intoxication gave way a little to prudence and reason. So she got out her curling irons and lighted the gas and went to work repairing the ravages made by generosity added to love. Which is always a tremendous task, dear friends—a mammoth task.

Within forty minutes her head was covered with tiny, close-lying curls that made her look wonderfully like a truant schoolboy. She looked at her reflection in the mirror long, carefully, and critically.

"If Jim doesn't kill me," she said to herself, "before he takes a second look at me, he'll say I look like a Coney Island chorus girl. But what could I do—oh! what could I do with a dollar and eighty-seven cents?"

At seven o'clock the coffee was made and the frying pan was on the back of the stove, hot and ready to cook the chops.

Jim was never late. Della doubled the watch chain in her hand and sat on the corner of the table near the door that he always entered. Then she heard his step on the stair away down on the first flight, and she turned white for just a moment. She had a habit of saying little silent prayers about the simplest everyday things, and now she whispered: "Please God, make him think I am still pretty."

The door opened and Jim stepped in and closed it. He looked thin and very serious. Poor fellow, he was only twenty-two—and to be burdened with a family! He needed a new overcoat and he was without gloves.

Jim stepped inside the door, as immovable as a setter at the scent of quail. His eyes were fixed upon Della, and there was an expression in them that she could not read, and it terrified her. It was not anger, nor surprise, nor disapproval, nor horror, nor any of the sentiments that

she had been prepared for. He simply stared at her fixedly with that peculiar expression on his face.

Della wriggled off the table and went for him.

"Jim, darling," she cried, "don't look at me that way. I had my hair cut off and sold it because I couldn't have lived through Christmas without giving you a present. It'll grow out again—you won't mind, will you? I just had to do it. My hair grows awfully fast. Say 'Merry Christmas!' Jim, and let's be happy. You don't know what a nice— what a beautiful, nice gift I've got for you."

"You've cut off your hair?" asked Jim, laboriously, as if he had not arrived at that patent fact yet even after the hardest mental labour.

"Cut it off and sold it," said Della. "Don't you like me just as well, anyhow? I'm me without my hair, ain't I?"

Jim looked about the room curiously.

"You say your hair is gone?" he said, with an air almost of idiocy.

"You needn't look for it," said Della. "It's sold, I tell you—sold and gone too. It's Christmas Eve, boy. Be good to me, for it went for you. Maybe the hairs of my head were numbered," she went on with a sudden serious sweetness, "but nobody could ever count my love for you. Shall I put the chops on, Jim?"

Out of his trance Jim seemed to quickly wake. He enfolded his Della. For ten seconds let us regard with discreet scrutiny some inconsequential object in the other direction. Eight dollars a week or a million a year—what's the difference? A mathematician or a wit would give you the wrong answer. The magi brought valuable gifts, but that was not among them. This dark assertion will be illuminated later on.

Jim drew a package from his overcoat pocket and threw it upon the table.

"Don't make any mistake, Dell," he said, "about me. I don't think there's anything in the way of a haircut or a shave or a shampoo that could make me like my girl any less. But if you'll unwrap that package you may see why you had me going awhile at first."

White fingers and nimble tore at the string and paper. And then an ecstatic scream of joy; and then, alas! a quick feminine change to hysterical tears and wails, necessitating the immediate employment of all the comforting powers of the lord of the flat.

For there lay The Combs—the set of combs, that Della had worshipped for long in a Broadway window. Beautiful combs, pure tortoiseshell with jewelled rims—just the shade to wear in the beautiful vanished hair. They were expensive combs, she knew, and her heart had simply craved and yearned over them without the least hope of possession. And now, they were hers, but the tresses that should have adorned the coveted adornments were gone.

But she hugged them to her bosom, and at length she was able to look up with dim eyes and a smile and say: "My hair grows so fast, Jim!"

And then Della leaped up like a little singed cat and cried, "Oh, oh!"

Jim had not yet seen his beautiful present. She held it out to him eagerly upon her open palm. The dull precious metal seemed to flash with a reflection of her bright and ardent spirit.

"Isn't it a dandy, Jim? I hunted all over town to find it. You'll have to look at the time a hundred times a day now. Give me your watch. I want to see how it looks on it."

Instead of obeying, Jim tumbled down on the couch and put his hands under the back of his head and smiled.

"Dell," said he, "let's put our Christmas presents away and keep 'em a while. They're too nice to use just at present. I sold the watch to get the money to buy your combs. And now suppose you put the chops on."

The magi, as you know, were wise men—wonderfully wise men—who brought gifts to the Babe in the manger. They invented the art of giving Christmas presents. Being wise, their gifts were no doubt wise ones, possibly bearing the privilege of exchange in case of duplication. And here I have lamely related to you the uneventful chronicle of two foolish children in a flat who most unwisely sacrificed for each other the greatest treasures of their house. But in a last word to the wise of these days, let it be said that of all who give gifts these two were the wisest. Of all who give and receive gifts, such as they are wisest. Everywhere they are wisest. They are the magi.

The Trapper's Christmas Eve

ROBERT W. SERVICE

It's mighty lonesome-like and drear.
Above the Wild the moon rides high,
And shows up sharp and needle-clear
The emptiness of earth and sky;
No happy homes with love aglow;
No Santa Claus to make-believe:
Just snow and snow, and then more snow;
It's Christmas Eve, it's Christmas Eve.

And here am I where all things end,
And Undesirables are hurled;
A poor old man without a friend,
Forgot and dead to all the world;
Clean out of sight and out of mind…
Well, maybe it is better so;
We all in life our level find,
And mine, I guess, is pretty low.

Yet as I sit with pipe alight
Beside the cabin fire, it's queer
This mind of mine must take tonight
The backwards trail of fifty year.
The schoolhouse and the Christmas tree;
The children with their cheeks aglow;
Two bright blue eyes that smile on me...
Just half a century ago.

Again (it's maybe forty years),
With faith and trust almost divine,
These same blue eyes, abrim with tears,
Through depths of love look into mine.
A parting, tender, soft and low,
With arms that cling and lips that cleave...
Ah me! it's all so long ago,
Yet seems so sweet this Christmas Eve.

Just thirty years ago, again...
We say a bitter, last goodbye;
Our lips are white with wrath and pain;
Our little children cling and cry.
Whose was the fault? It matters not,
For man and woman both deceive;
It's buried now and all forgot,
Forgiven, too, this Christmas Eve.

And she (God pity me) is dead;
Our children men and women grown.
I like to think that they are wed,
With little children of their own,
That crowd around their Christmas tree...
I would not ever have them grieve,
Or shed a single tear for me,
To mar their joy this Christmas Eve.

Stripped to the buff and gaunt and still
Lies all the land in grim distress.
Like lost soul wailing, long and shrill,
A wolf howl cleaves the emptiness.
Then hushed as Death is everything.
The moon rides haggard and forlorn...
"O hark the herald angels sing!"
God bless all men—it's Christmas morn.

The First Christmas Tree

EUGENE FIELD

Once upon a time the forest was in a great commotion. Early in the evening the wise old cedars had shaken their heads ominously and predicted strange things. They had lived in the forest many, many years; but never had they seen such marvellous sights as were to be seen now in the sky, and upon the hills, and in the distant village.

"Pray tell us what you see," pleaded a little vine. "We who are not as tall as you can behold none of these wonderful things. Describe them to us, that we may enjoy them with you."

"I am filled with such amazement," said one of the cedars, "that I can hardly speak. The whole sky seems to be aflame, and the stars appear to be dancing among the clouds; angels walk down from heaven to the earth, and enter the village or talk with the shepherds upon the hills."

The vine listened in mute astonishment. Such things never before had happened. The vine trembled with excitement. Its nearest neighbour was a tiny tree, so small it scarcely ever was noticed; yet it was a very beautiful little tree, and the vines and ferns and mosses and other humble residents of the forest loved it dearly.

"How I should like to see the angels!" sighed the little tree, "and how I should like to see the stars dancing among the clouds! It must be very beautiful."

As the vine and the little tree talked of these things, the cedars watched with increasing interest the wonderful scenes over and beyond the confines of the forest. Presently they thought they heard music, and they were not mistaken, for soon the whole air was full of the sweetest harmonies ever heard upon earth.

"What beautiful music!" cried the little tree. "I wonder whence it comes."

"The angels are singing," said a cedar, "for none but angels could make such sweet music."

"But the stars are singing too," said another cedar, "yes, and the shepherds on the hills join in the song, and what a strangely glorious song it is!"

The trees listened to the singing, but they did not understand its meaning: it seemed to be an anthem, and it was of a Child that had been born; but further than this they did not understand. The strange and glorious song continued all the night; and all that night the angels walked to and fro, and the shepherd-folk talked with the angels, and the stars danced and carolled in high heaven. And it was nearly morning when the cedars cried out, "They are coming to the forest! The angels are coming to the forest!" And, surely enough, this was true. The vine and the little tree were very terrified, and they begged their older and stronger neighbours to protect them from harm. But the cedars were too busy with their own fears to pay any heed to the faint pleadings of the humble vine and the little tree. The angels came into the forest, singing the same glorious anthem about the Child, and the stars sang in chorus with them, until every part of the woods rang with echoes of that wondrous song.

There was nothing in the appearance of this angel host to inspire

fear; they were clad all in white, and there were crowns upon their fair heads, and golden harps in their hands; love, hope, charity, compassion, and joy beamed from their beautiful faces, and their presence seemed to fill the forest with a divine peace. The angels came through the forest to where the little tree stood, and gathering around it, they touched it with their hands, and kissed its little branches, and sang even more sweetly than before. And their song was about the Child, the Child, the Child that had been born. Then the stars came down from the skies and danced and hung upon the branches of the tree, and they too sang that song—the song of the Child. And all the other trees and the vines and the ferns and the mosses beheld in wonder; nor could they understand why all these things were being done, and why this exceeding honour should be shown the little tree.

When the morning came the angels left the forest—all but one angel, who remained behind and lingered near the little tree. Then a cedar asked: "Why do you tarry with us, holy angel?"

And the angel answered: "I stay to guard this little tree, for it is sacred, and no harm shall come to it."

The little tree felt quite relieved by this assurance, and it held up its head more confidently than ever before. And how it thrived and grew, and waxed in strength and beauty! The cedars said they never had seen the like. The sun seemed to lavish its choicest rays upon the little tree, heaven dropped its sweetest dew upon it, and the winds never came to the forest that they did not forget their rude manners and linger to kiss the little tree and sing it their prettiest songs. No danger ever menaced it, no harm threatened; for the angel never slept—through the day and through the night the angel watched the little tree and protected it from all evil. Oftentimes the trees talked with the angel; but of course they understood little of what he said, for he spoke always of the Child who was to become the Master; and always when thus he talked, he caressed the little tree, and stroked its branches and leaves, and moistened them with his tears. It all was so very strange that none in the forest could understand.

So the years passed, the angel watching his blooming charge. Sometimes the beasts strayed toward the little tree and threatened to devour its tender foliage; sometimes the woodman came with his axe, intent upon hewing down the straight and comely thing; sometimes the hot, consuming breath of drought swept from the south, and sought to blight the forest and all its verdure: the angel kept them from the little tree. Serene and beautiful it grew, until now it was no longer a little tree, but the pride and glory of the forest.

One day the tree heard someone coming through the forest. Hitherto the angel had hastened to its side when men approached; but now the angel strode away and stood under the cedars yonder.

"Dear angel," cried the tree, "can you not hear the footsteps of someone approaching? Why do you leave me?"

"Have no fear," said the angel, "for He who comes is the Master."

The Master came to the tree and beheld it. He placed His hands upon its smooth trunk and branches, and the tree was thrilled with a strange and glorious delight. Then He stooped and kissed the tree, and then He turned and went away.

Many times after that the Master came to the forest, and when He came it always was to where the tree stood. Many times He rested beneath the tree and enjoyed the shade of its foliage, and listened to the music of the wind as it swept through the rustling leaves. Many times He slept there, and the tree watched over Him, and the forest was still, and all its voices were hushed. And the angel hovered near like a faithful sentinel.

Ever and anon men came with the Master to the forest, and sat with Him in the shade of the tree, and talked with Him of matters which the tree never could understand; only it heard that the talk was of love and charity and gentleness, and it saw that the Master was beloved and venerated by the others. It heard them tell of the Master's goodness and humility—how He had healed the sick and raised the dead and bestowed inestimable blessings wherever He walked. And the

tree loved the Master for His beauty and His goodness; and when He came to the forest it was full of joy, but when He came not it was sad. And the other trees of the forest joined in its happiness and its sorrow, for they too loved the Master. And the angel always hovered near.

The Master came one night alone into the forest, and His face was pale with anguish and wet with tears, and He fell upon His knees and prayed. The tree heard Him, and all the forest was still, as if it were standing in the presence of death. And when the morning came, lo! the angel had gone.

Then there was a great confusion in the forest. There was a sound of rude voices, and a clashing of swords and staves. Strange men appeared, uttering loud oaths and cruel threats, and the tree was filled with terror. It called aloud for the angel, but the angel came not.

"Alas," cried the vine, "they have come to destroy the tree, the pride and glory of the forest!"

The forest was sorely agitated, but it was in vain. The strange men plied their axes with cruel vigour, and the tree was hewn to the ground. Its beautiful branches were cut away and cast aside, and its soft, thick foliage was strewn to the tenderer mercies of the winds.

"They are killing me!" cried the tree, "Why is not the angel here to protect me?"

But no one heard the piteous cry—none but the other trees of the forest; and they wept, and the little vine wept too.

Then the cruel men dragged the despoiled and hewn tree from the forest, and the forest saw that beauteous thing no more.

But the night wind that swept down from the City of the Great King that night to ruffle the bosom of distant Galilee, tarried in the forest awhile to say that it had seen that day a cross upraised on Calvary—the tree on which was stretched the body of the dying Master.

A Tribute to Alan Maitland

Alan Maitland joined the Canadian Broadcasting Corporation as an announcer in 1947. Through the following years, he appeared on many programs, including *Fresh Air*, *The Nature of Things*, and *Eclectic Circus*. He was best known as the co-host of *As It Happens*, a position he held for nearly twenty years. Also known as Fireside Al and later Front Porch Al, he was best loved for his readings of enchanting stories during the holiday season. In 1980, he and Barbara Frum shared an ACTRA award for Best Public Affairs Broadcasters. He retired from the CBC in 1993 and died in 1999 at the age of 78 after a long illness. Alan Maitland had his last CBC on-air performance at the thirtieth anniversary of *As It Happens* in 1998. He will long be remembered for his warm, resonant voice and his ability to draw people into the story he was reading.

Canadian Broadcasting Corporation